HUG IT OUT!

Louis Thomas

FARRAR STRAUS GIROUX
New York

Farrar Straus Giroux Books for Young Readers
An imprint of Macmillan Publishing Group, LLC
175 Fifth Avenue, New York 10010

Copyright © 2017 by Louis Thomas
All rights reserved
Color separations by Embassy Graphics
Printed in the United States of America
by Phoenix Color, Hagerstown, Maryland
First edition, 2017
1 3 5 7 9 10 8 6 4 2

mackids.com

Library of Congress Cataloging-in-Publication Data

Names: Thomas, Louis, 1987– author, illustrator.
Title: Hug it out! / Louis Thomas.
Description: First edition. | New York : Farrar Straus Giroux, 2017. | Summary: Tired of hearing
  her son and daughter fight, Mom devises an unusual punishment.
Identifiers: LCCN 2015036150 | ISBN 9780374303143 (hardback)
Subjects: | CYAC: Brothers and sisters—Fiction. | Quarreling—Fiction. | Hugging—Fiction. |
  BISAC: JUVENILE FICTION / Family / Siblings. | JUVENILE FICTION / Humorous Stories.
Classification: LCC PZ7.1.T465 Hu 2016 | DDC [E]—dc23
LC record available at https://lccn.loc.gov/2015036150

Our books may be purchased in bulk for promotional, educational, or business use. Please
contact your local bookseller or the Macmillan Corporate and Premium Sales Department at
(800) 221-7945 ext. 5442 or by e-mail at MacmillanSpecialMarkets@macmillan.com.

To my parents, with hugs
—L.T.

It was a rainy Sunday afternoon. Woody and Annie were playing inside.

Woody was making an airport. *Zoooom! Screeech!*
Annie was building a town. *Good morning, everyone!*

Everything was perfect. Until . . .

. . . they both reached for the car.

"Hey! That's mine," Woody said. He wanted the car to pick up travelers from his airport.

"No way! It's MINE," Annie said. She needed the car to cruise through her town.

"Mom!" Woody called.

"MOM!" Annie called louder.

"You kids need to share," their mother said.

"Okay," promised Woody.

"We will," added Annie. And they pinkie swore on it.

"Good," said their mother.

But sharing had never worked for Annie and Woody.

"Hey! You've had it for long enough!"
"No way! It's only been a minute!"
"You dumb-dumb!"
"You ding-dong!"

"Mommm! Woody called me a ding-dong!" Annie yelled.
"Well, she called me a dumb-dumb first!" Woody yelled
louder.

"You kids need to apologize to each other," their mother said.

"I'm sorry," mumbled Annie.

"Me too," whispered Woody.

"You're not a dumb-dumb."

"And you're not a ding-dong. Well, not a *big* one, anyway."

"Okay," said their mother. "Good enough."

But after apologizing, there almost always
came a round of kicking.

"Ow! Quit it!"
"Stop! That hurt!"
"Mommmm!" called Annie.
"Mommmm!" screamed Woody.

"Mom

"That's IT!" their mother yelled back.
"I'm sick and tired of you two fighting!
From now on, any time you argue, you're
going to have to . . .

. . . HUG IT OUT."

"Hug it what?"
"Hug it who?"
"Hug it how?"
"Hug it huh?"

"Hug it OUT,"
Mom said again.

"Now get together . . .

. . . AND HUG!"

But this new punishment was hard to remember. (Especially when all Woody and Annie wanted was to forget it!)

"Hug it out!"

"Hug it out!"

"Hug it out!"

"HUG. IT. OUT!"

"I can't take even one more hug," Annie finally admitted.

"Me neither," sighed Woody. "I'm as flat as a pancake!"

"What are we gonna do?" Annie wondered.

"Um, can you give me a little space to think?" Woody asked.

So they took some time apart.

Woody played with his planes.

They traveled from Paris to Rome, and crossed the ocean to New York.

Annie played with her town.
She delivered papers, put out a fire, and rescued pets.

And they both found a way to play with the car.

In fact, they'd been playing happily on their own for so long that they *almost* didn't notice they hadn't hugged in a while.

"Hey, Annie?" Woody said. "I kind of miss . . ."
"You," Annie finished.
"Do you want to . . . ?" Woody asked.

"Mommmm!" Annie screamed.
"Mommmm!" Woody screamed louder.

"HUG IT OUT!" their mother yelled back.

And they did.

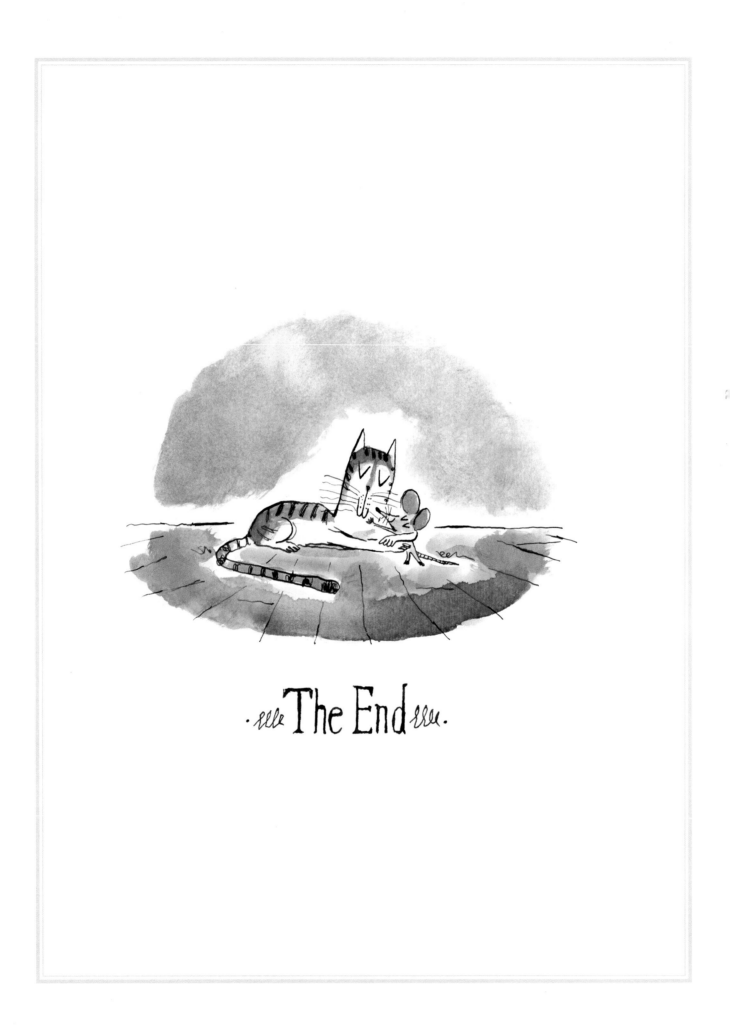

The End.